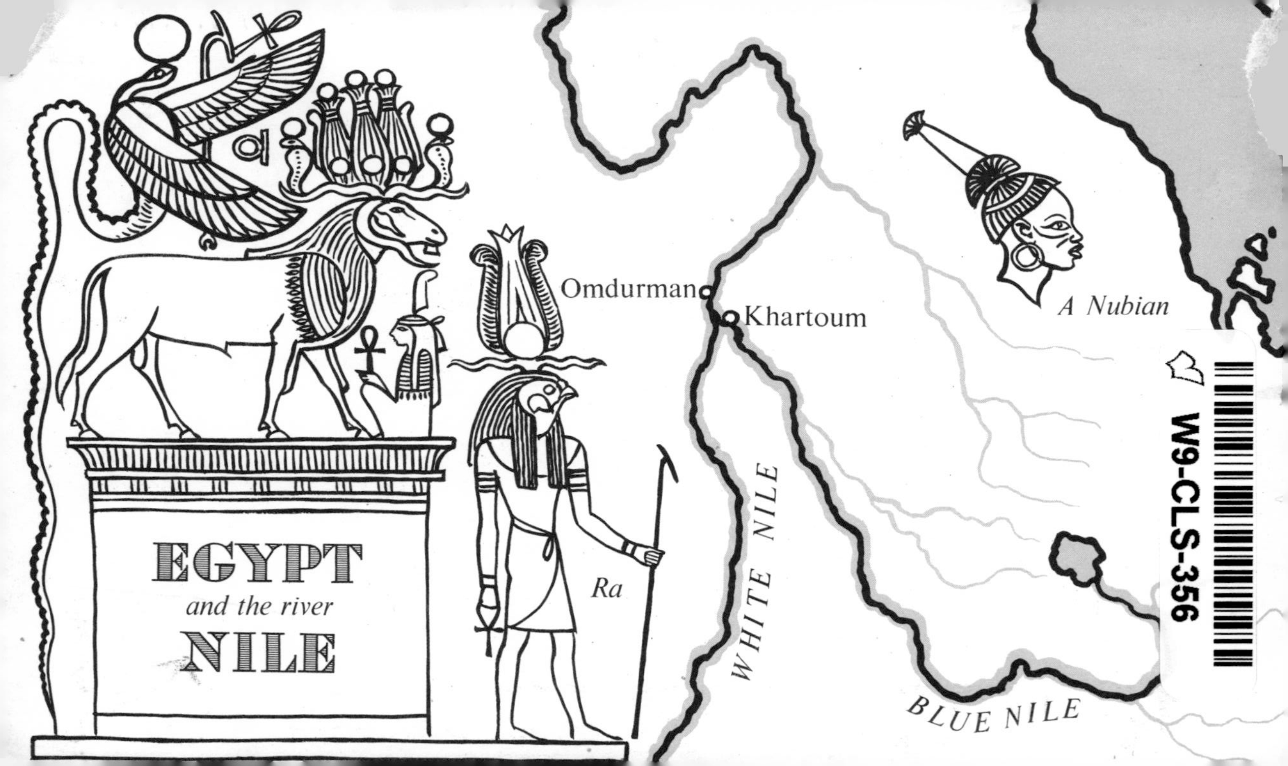
EGYPT
and the river
NILE
Ra
Omdurman
Khartoum
A Nubian
WHITE NILE
BLUE NILE

Series 561

Everyone has heard of Cleopatra: this book tells something of one of the oldest countries in the world, over which she ruled.

Cleopatra and Ancient Egypt

by L. DU GARDE PEACH, M.A., Ph.D., D.Litt.

with illustrations by JOHN KENNEY

Ladybird Books Loughborough

CLEOPATRA and ANCIENT EGYPT

Five thousand years ago, the Stone Age men were living in Britain. You can read all about them in another book in this series: how they lived in caves and wore clothes made of the skins of the animals which they hunted with weapons made of sharp-edged flints.

Far away in Egypt, at the same time, other people were living in great cities, building wonderful temples, wearing rich clothes and jewels, with merchants in their shops, soldiers on their horses, and lawyers sitting in the courts of justice.

These people were the Egyptians, and we know a great deal about them because people called archaeologists have found on scrolls, or on the walls of tombs, pictures and writings describing their lives and buildings.

The Egyptians had a very strange way of writing called hieroglyphics.* It was all done in pictures, and for a long time the archaeologists were unable to read it. Then one day a French scholar found a stone on which the same inscription had been carved both in Greek and in the picture language of the Egyptians. As he knew Greek, he was able to read the picture writing. This stone is called the Rosetta Stone, from the place where it was found, and it is from this beginning that we can now read the ancient Egyptian writing.

**Pronounced* hire-o-gliff-icks

All writing was done by the priests, and as paper had not been invented, they used the stems of a plant called papyrus. It is from this that we get the word 'paper' to-day.

The stem of the plant was cut into long thin strips, which were placed side by side. Other strips were then placed across them, woven over and under, to make a sort of mat. This was soaked in water, which made the two layers stick together, and the papyrus mat was hammered on a flat stone. Finally, after being dried in the sun, it was rubbed quite smooth with a piece of ivory. It was then ready for use.

These sheets of papyrus were often joined together to make long rolls, called scrolls, and were not bound like the books which we have to-day. The scroll was wound on two wooden rollers, and as it was read, it was rolled from one roller to the other. This must have been much more difficult than just turning the pages of a book.

The priests used coloured inks and pens made from grass or straw, and some of the papyrus scrolls which have been found are very beautifully drawn and coloured.

The Egyptians were wonderful builders, and long before Stonehenge was built in Britain, they had raised great temples to the many gods of their religion. Some of these temples are still to be seen in Egypt at places like Karnak, where the great Hall of Columns stands to-day where it was built thousands of years ago.

They also carved statues of the rulers, who were called Pharaohs.† Near Thebes are the two great figures of a Pharaoh named Amenhotep,* and in ancient times, as the sun rose each morning, musical notes could be heard coming from one of them. The people thought they were the voice of the statue greeting the sun.

All over Egypt are to be found statues and paintings on the walls of the temples, representing the gods. Some of these gods were very strange. One of them was shown with the body of a man and the head of a hawk. He was called Ra at first, but was later worshipped as Ammon-Ra.

Ra was the god of the sun and was one of the most important gods. The Egyptians pictured him sailing his boat across the sky each day, from east to west, bringing light and life to the people of the Nile.

 †*Pronounced* Fair-ohs *Pronounced* Ar-men-ho-tep

The best known of all the monuments of ancient Egypt are the pyramids and the Sphinx at Gizeh, near Cairo.

The Great Pyramid is a solid building of great blocks of stone, covering thirteen acres of land, and one hundred and fifty feet higher than St. Paul's Cathedral. The base is square, and the sides were so carefully measured that they are within an inch of being exactly the same length. They slope inwards, meeting in a point at the top.

This pyramid was built by a Pharaoh named Cheops, who reigned in Egypt about five thousand years ago. Far in the interior of the pyramid is his burial chamber, reached by a long, narrow passage. Thousands of slaves were employed for twenty years quarrying and carting the stone for this great tomb.

Equally famous is the Sphinx, a figure of a lion with a human head. This stands close to the Great Pyramid, is one hundred and eighty nine feet long, and hewn out of the living rock. It was probably already there when the Great Pyramid was built, though some Egyptologists, as the people who study the ancient monuments of Egypt are called, think that it was made at the same time. This Sphinx is so big that there was once a temple between its paws.

We have seen that the pyramids were carefully built. The master masons must have been very exact in their measurements, not only of the size of the stones but also of the angle of the sloping sides of the pyramids. In the picture you see one of them measuring a block with a piece of string.

The blocks of stone for the pyramid of Khufu came from the other side of the river Nile, and the labour of moving them was very great. The workmen probably used long levers of tough wood to lift them a little at a time, so that they could put rollers underneath. They were then dragged by hundreds of slaves pulling on long ropes made of twisted leather.

In a tomb of a local governor named Zhut-hotep* there is a picture of a great statue being moved by this method, and on the statue a man is standing, clapping his hands as a signal to the slaves to pull all together.

The stones were all shaped with copper chisels, later replaced by bronze and iron tools. The Egyptians did not possess the big cranes and engines which we have to-day. Even with these the building of a pyramid as large as that of Khufu would be a large undertaking.

**Pronounced* Zoot-ho-tep

We speak of the various rulers of ancient Egypt as belonging to different dynasties. There were many dynasties, usually consisting of rulers who were descended from the same family. Sometimes a Pharaoh had no child to succeed him, or sometimes the ruler of some other race would conquer Egypt, and found a new dynasty.

The greatest dynasties of all were the eighteenth and nineteenth, the Pharaohs of which reigned from about 1650 to 1280 B.C. This long period of nearly four hundred years, a period as long as that from the reign of Queen Elizabeth I to to-day, is called the New Empire. The reign of the first Pharaoh of the Eighteenth Dynasty marked a new beginning for Egypt, as he was the ruler who drove out the foreigners who had ruled the country for four hundred and fifty years.

The greatest of these Pharaohs was Thothmes* III. He conquered the countries adjacent to Egypt, from far into the Libyan desert in the west, to the river Tigris in the east. Many wall paintings show him in his chariot, victoriously riding down his enemies. It was Thothmes III who caused to be made the obelisk, wrongly called Cleopatra's Needle, which now stands on the Embankment in London.

*_Pronounced_ Thoth-mees

Many of the Pharaohs of these two dynasties were great soldiers and conquerors. The picture on the opposite page shows one of them returning to Egypt in triumph after a victorious campaign.

In the wall paintings in the tombs of these Pharaohs we can see pictures of such triumphs, where the chariot of the conqueror is followed by hundreds of prisoners. These would either be put to death or sold as slaves. No doubt many of them were made to work for the rest of their lives on the building of the tombs and temples of their masters.

There were two great Pharaohs of the Nineteenth Dynasty. One was Seti* I. It was he who built the Hall of Columns at Karnak, and cut the most elaborate of the tombs in the rock of the Valley of Tombs near Thebes.

Rameses II, the other great Pharaoh, reigned for sixty-seven years, and among many outstanding works he constructed a canal from the Nile to the Red Sea. He it was who received and honoured Joseph, and it was under his son, Menephtha, that the Jews were driven out of Egypt. It is the story of this which we read in the Bible, in Genesis and Exodus, and in the Book of Numbers.

**Pronounced* Setty

Under Rameses II Egypt was a great and powerful nation, and to it came the products of Africa and the countries at the far end of the Mediterranean. In the tomb pictures we see many strange animals, as well as elephants, giraffes, leopards and monkeys, all being brought as tribute to the great Pharaoh.

Overland from the east came rich jewels from India, spices and frankincense and myrrh from Persia, and perhaps silks over the long trail from China. Gold and silver poured into the treasure houses of Egypt, and the richness of the offerings placed in the tombs of the Pharaohs shows that in the making of jewelled ornaments and decorated furniture, the craftsmen of ancient Egypt have never been surpassed.

When tribute came to Egypt from the conquered countries, it was the custom to parade it through the streets in procession. This was to show all the people how great and powerful was the Pharaoh who ruled over them.

The peasants in Egypt were practically slaves. They could be bought or sold with the land, and as there was no money in Egypt, they possessed nothing. They were given enough to keep them alive, that was all.

The richly decorated costumes and the fabulous jewels worn by a Pharaoh and his queen, were very different from the miserable rags worn by the peasants. Wall paintings show us exactly how they dressed, and so many things have been preserved in the dry air of Upper Egypt, that we can see and handle the actual ornaments, and sometimes even the clothes of ancient Egypt.

Not that they wore very much. Egypt is a very hot country, and often even the Pharaoh is pictured as wearing nothing but a sort of little apron. He made up for the lack of clothing with richly jewelled and enamelled necklaces and bracelets.

Most interesting is the double crown worn by the Pharaoh on ceremonial occasions. In the earliest times Upper and Lower Egypt were two different countries, and each had a ceremonial head-dress for its ruler. When the two countries joined together, thousands of years ago, the two crowns were made into one.

The crown of Upper Egypt was tall and white, with a bulbous knob on top; that of Lower Egypt was red and very peculiar in shape. In the picture you can see what they looked like when they were combined.

Because Egypt was such a rich country, there were many wealthy people. As the ladies of the court and the wives of rich men did no work, they spent much of their time making themselves look beautiful.

During the long history of ancient Egypt fashions changed very much. However, it would seem from the dressing-table ornaments which have been preserved, that Egyptian women used a lot of make-up. Rouge pots, sometimes even with rouge in them, and eyebrow pencils, powder boxes and scent bottles, beautifully decorated metal mirrors and combs, are to be seen in the British Museum in London.

Women to-day spend a lot of time on dressing their hair: so did the Egyptian women. But instead of arranging their own hair, they often cut it short and wore elaborate wigs, the form and shape of which changed from time to time.

The picture shows an Egyptian lady making up her eyes, with her slaves in attendance. She is probably painting a green line under the eyes, and her eyelids and eyebrows black, to make them appear larger and more brilliant. On the table beside her is a jar with sweet smelling oil made of frankincense and myrrh.

A rich banquet in the time of Rameses II, three thousand years ago, must have been a very colourful occasion. The Egyptians were very civilised people, and the wall paintings show us that they were also well behaved.

In early times the Egyptians sat on the ground at meals, but by the Nineteenth Dynasty, about 1650 to 1400 B.C., they sat on cushioned chairs, and the small tables were decorated with lotus flowers. Jars of wine were also wreathed with flowers, and the guests wore flowers in their hair.

We have an account of a banquet at which there were ten different sorts of meat, five different birds, and sixteen kinds of bread and cake. There was an abundance of fruit and great jars of wine. Everything was served on silver dishes, and the little loaves were made in a variety of fancy shapes.

During the meal the guests were entertained by musicians, playing pipes and flutes, trumpets and harps. Many of these instruments are in museums, and we are able to play music heard by the Egyptians thousands of years ago, using the very same instruments on which they played. The musicians, and sometimes the guests, had on their heads cones of sweet-smelling wax which melted and ran down into their hair.

In many of the tombs are found little clay or wooden models of the houses in which the Egyptians lived, so we know exactly what they were like.

They were often of two stories, with balconies over which were brightly coloured awnings. There was no glass in the windows, because in the very hot climate of Upper Egypt it was pleasant to have a cool breeze blowing through the house. Roofs were flat, just as they are in Cairo to-day.

The houses of the richer people had beautifully carved and decorated tables and chairs. There were coloured mats on the walls and soft rugs on the floor. Everything about the house, inside and out, was brightly painted, and many of the houses were surrounded by gardens in which grew palm and fig trees, grape vines and all kinds of flowering shrubs.

The houses of the poor were very different. These were usually single rooms built of mud bricks, dried in the sun, without any of the colours or furniture as in the houses of the rich Egyptians. Such houses may still be seen in any Egyptian village to-day; they have probably altered very little since the days of the Pharaohs.

We have seen that the Egyptians were great builders of pyramids and tombs and temples. In addition to the thousands of men employed in erecting these enormous buildings, there were all the carpenters and brickmakers, the painters and plasterers, the gardeners and decorators employed in building the houses in which the people lived.

The wall paintings and the papyrus scrolls show us many of these people at work. We can see the brickmakers shaping the bricks in wooden moulds and baking them in the sun. With these bricks they built walls sometimes as much as eighty feet thick.

The carpenters had many of the tools, such as chisels and saws, which we have to-day. But where a modern carpenter makes joints, they would sometimes train a tree for years to form right-angled pieces of wood. They even made a three legged stool by training three branches in the right directions and cutting the seat out of the trunk between them.

The pottery and glass-ware makers, and the gold and silver smiths, were skilled craftsmen, and museums all over the world have beautiful specimens of their work. Coloured stones, such as red porphyry and semi-precious amethysts, were used for many decorative purposes.

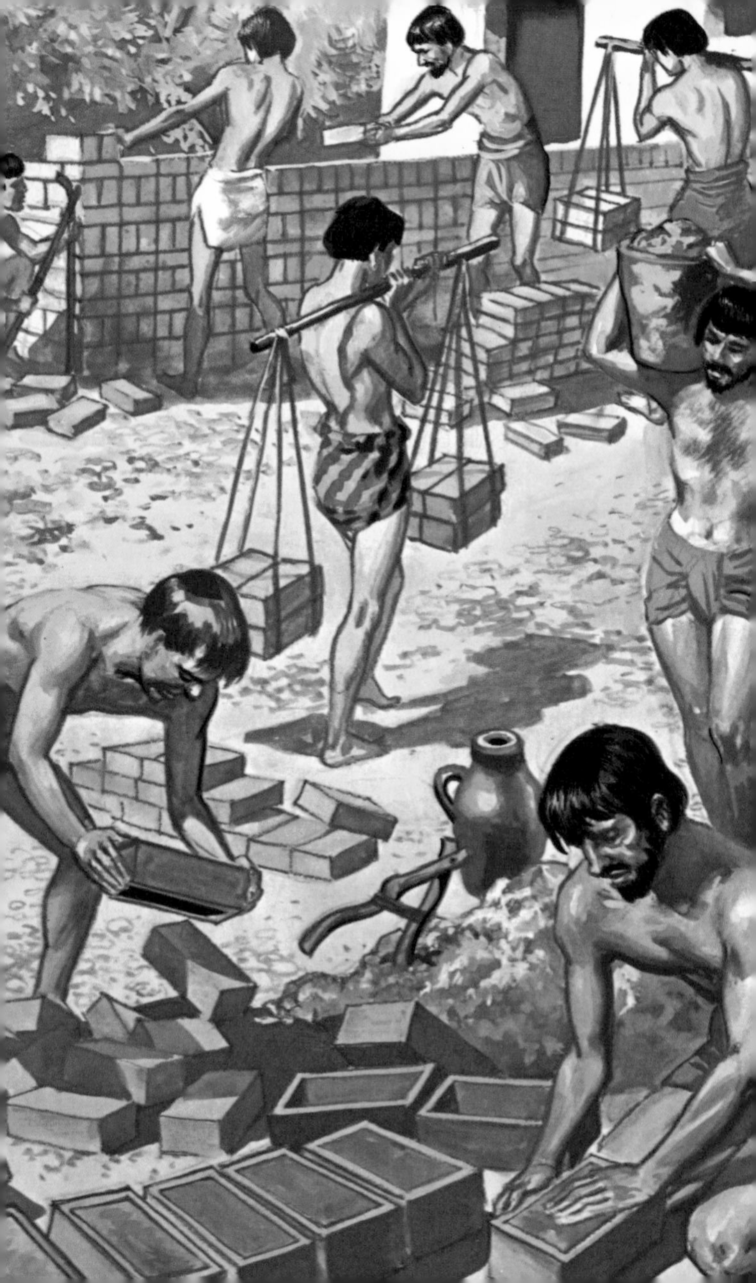

The Egyptians were mainly farmers, but theirs was a peculiar kind of farming depending, as it still does in Egypt to-day, on the water of the river Nile.

We have seen that Egypt is a long, narrow strip of country along the course of the Nile, with barren deserts to east and west. If it were not for the river, Egypt could not exist. Every year during the summer, after the heavy tropical rains in central Africa, the Nile brings down the water needed to irrigate the land, parched during the hot weather.

Sometimes the rains fail, and this always used to mean a famine in Egypt. But to-day a very large dam has been built to store the water in times of heavy rains, and so avoid the danger of famine.

The ancient Egyptian farmer had very little to do. His harvest depended on the Nile flooding the land. He lightly ploughed the soil and scattered the seed; sometimes he even sowed the seed without ploughing, and turned herds of pigs on to the land to tread it in. After that, all he had to do was to gather in the harvest. No wonder the ancient Egyptians worshipped the Nile as a god.

The Nile not only gave the Egyptian the rich land for his harvest, it served him in many other ways. It was his chief means of getting from one part of Egypt to another, and by fishing in it he procured a large part of his daily food.

For these purposes he needed boats, and from the earliest times the Egyptians made little canoes by hollowing out the trunks of trees. But by the time of Rameses, they had learnt how to build wooden boats with large triangular sails and oars. In the tombs of the Pharaohs were found beautifully made models of these boats, with the rowers in their places and the steersman with his large oar at the stern.

Similar boats may be seen on the Nile to-day. When travelling down the stream they use their sails, but up stream the rowers have to pull hard against the current.

The Egyptians fished either from these boats or from the shore. They can still be seen to-day fishing as they did when Rameses ruled the land. A boat takes a long, narrow net out into the river in a semi-circle, each end being held on land. Then when the net is drawn in from the two ends, all the fish which have swum into it are pulled ashore.

By the time the Egyptians had reached the high civilisation of the Nineteenth Dynasty, there were many things which they required and which had to be imported from other countries.

In the days of the early dynasties, seven or even eight thousand years ago, such trade as existed in Egypt was chiefly across the desert from Nubia. The Egyptians lived mostly in Upper Egypt and knew very little about the sea or the lands beyond it.

By the time of Rameses they had combined Upper and Lower Egypt, and peopled the delta of the Nile. They were now on the coast of the Mediterranean, and became familiar with the ocean-going ships of the Phoenicians and the hardy sailors from Crete. They decided to build ships of their own.

We have many models of these ships, often found in the tombs of the kings. They are brightly coloured, with decorated bows, often in the form of the lotus flower. They have single sails, large to catch the faintest breeze over the desert; when the wind failed, the ships were rowed by slaves, many of whom were prisoners taken in war. The ships were well built for the work which they had to do, sailing up and down the Nile.

When a Pharaoh or some important court official died, there were many ceremonies which had to be performed. It is because of this, and because the tombs were so carefully painted with scenes of the daily lives of the people, that we know so much about them.

The body of the Pharaoh was wrapped in many yards of linen and then placed in a wooden case, made to represent him. These cases, some of which can be seen in the British Museum, were painted in bright colours and the face was carefully carved. They have even been found covered with thinly beaten sheets of solid gold.

This carved case was then placed inside another, similarly carved, and this again inside a third. All the time the priests were reading from the sacred books, and the ceremony of preparing the body of the Pharaoh for his tomb could last as long as seventy days.

Finally the large case was placed on a sledge, drawn by a number of slaves. Often it was carried across the river Nile in a special boat. Finally it was laid in a pyramid, or in a tomb carved out of the rock, and the entrance was sealed.

In Egypt there is a grim, rocky valley, with no trace of trees or green grass. The sides are steep cliffs and great boulders lie on the sandy ground. It is the Valley of the Tombs.

In the rocks on each side are the tombs of Pharaohs and high officials. These were carved out of the rock by workmen whose only light was that of dim oil lamps. In spite of this, the walls of the tombs are carved and painted with great skill.

As many rich offerings were always placed in the tombs, they were often robbed, sometimes by the men who had constructed them, and soldiers were set to guard the narrow entrances to the valley. The Egyptians even went to the length of moving the bodies of Pharaohs secretly from one tomb to another to foil the robbers.

It is very rare to find a tomb which has not been robbed, but in 1922 one was discovered still containing all the wonderful treasures which had been placed in it more than three thousand years ago. It was the tomb of the young Pharaoh Tut-ankh-amen,* and a wonderful book has been published with pictures of the hundreds of things which it contained.

**Pronounced* Too-tan-kar-men

The tomb of Tut-ankh-amen was discovered by accident. It was below that of another Pharaoh, and when this was robbed, the rubble which the robbers dug out, completely hid the lower entrance.

It was in November, 1922, that the tomb of Tut-ankh-amen was uncovered. No-one had entered it for three thousand two hundred and sixty-five years, and almost all the treasures buried with a Pharaoh were found intact.

When anyone died, the Egyptians believed that he went to another world where he lived a life exactly like the one which he had lived on earth. So everything he would need was placed in the tomb with him. In the case of a royal Pharaoh it was of course very richly decorated. Furniture was inlaid with gold and precious stones, and such things as bowls and drinking cups were of solid gold, very beautifully designed.

The treasures from the tomb of Tut-ankh-amen are in the Museum in Cairo, and they give us a wonderful idea of how the Egyptians lived more than three thousand years ago. Some of these are shown in the picture opposite, but it is impossible to show them all. As we look at them, it is queer to remember what life was like here in Britain when these things were made.

All the wall paintings in the tombs, and the decorated scrolls and furniture, show that the ancient Egyptians were very skilled artists.

Their art was of a very particular kind, and to-day seems very strange to us. At the same time, it is very decorative, as the reproductions of many of the paintings clearly show. For instance, a row of slaves or soldiers, were all drawn exactly alike, often one behind the other. Also, they were nearly always drawn side-faced, even when the body was drawn as from the front, but the eyes were always as seen full-face. Feet and legs were almost always drawn from the side, and both as from the inner side of the foot, probably to avoid the difficulty of drawing the toes.

However, when the Egyptians made a statue, or carved a face on a sarcophagus (the name given to the case enclosing a body), they made it very life-like indeed.

One of the most beautiful statues which has been preserved is the head of Queen Nefertiti. It is made of stone and painted in a very life-like way, even the eyes look perfectly natural. This head shows that the Egyptian artists could have made natural looking drawings if they had so wished.

The Egyptian builders were able to build to very exact measurements, as in the case of the great pyramid of Khufu. This was because they understood arithmetic and geometry, although in a very primitive way. In the British Museum there is a very interesting scroll which contains a number of problems in arithmetic. Most of these are very practical: how to reckon the size of a field, or to find out how much grain would go into the bee-hive shaped granaries in the picture.

The Egyptians studied the stars, and all those thousands of years ago they worked out a calendar on which is based the one we use to-day. In some ways their calendar was more sensible than ours, because each month had the same number of days.

When the Egyptians were ill they could send for a doctor. Charms and prayers to the gods, together with a mixture of herbs, were often the remedy prescribed, but although they did not have all the medicines which we know to-day, they were skilful surgeons.

Life in ancient Egypt was not unhappy. They played games like chess, and ball games of various sorts. The children had their fairy tales, two of which, Cinderella, and The Forty Thieves, are still with us.

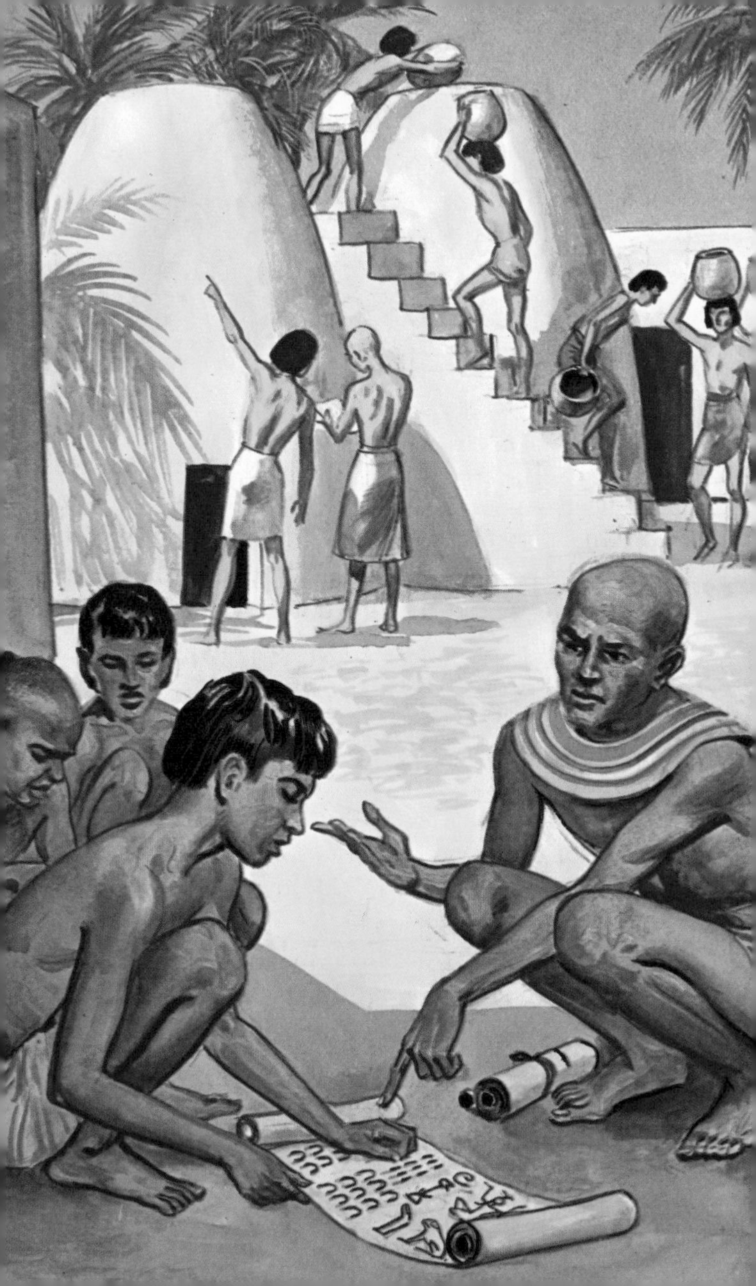

When we speak of ancient Egypt, most people think of Cleopatra. This is because so many stories and plays have been written about her, including one by Shakespeare.

Cleopatra does not really belong to ancient Egypt at all. From the time of Rameses, which we have been describing, nearly thirteen hundred years passed before Cleopatra was born, about the year 68 B.C.

In another book in this series you can read about Alexander the Great. He was a Macedonian, and after he had conquered Egypt in the year 332 B.C., one of his generals, named Ptolemy, became the ruler of the country and started a new dynasty. Cleopatra was the last of his descendants to rule in Egypt.

When she was only seventeen years of age Cleopatra became Queen of Egypt jointly with her brother, but it was not easy for a young girl to rule a country, and soon she was driven out and went to Syria to raise an army. Her intention was to recover the throne, and in this she was helped by Julius Caesar, who came to Egypt with a legion of Roman soldiers. The meeting of Caesar and Cleopatra altered the course of history. She was replaced on the throne by a younger brother, but when he was poisoned, she became the sole ruler of Egypt.

When Julius Caesar was assassinated Cleopatra was on a visit to Rome. Because she was a foreigner, she was not liked by the Roman people, so she returned to Egypt. There she lived as the Pharaohs before her had lived, in great splendour.

Julius Caesar had been succeeded by Octavius, and when Octavius quarrelled with Mark Anthony, who had been a friend of Caesar, Mark Anthony fled to Egypt. Octavius at once declared war on Egypt, and sailed with a great fleet of ships determined to destroy his enemy.

Mark Anthony also had a number of ships, and when he was joined by the ships of the Egyptians, he had more than Octavius. He sailed to meet him, confident of victory.

Mark Anthony was a better soldier than Octavius, and if he had fought him on land he would probably have won. Instead of this, he very unwisely met him at sea, off the west coast of Greece, near Actium. Even here he would probably have beaten Octavius, but in the middle of the battle Cleopatra, who was in a ship watching the fight, suddenly set sail for Egypt. Her ships followed her, and the battle was lost. Anthony and Cleopatra returned to Egypt.

Octavius followed, determined to kill Anthony and conquer Egypt. Anthony might even yet have beaten Octavius, but his army had lost faith in him when he fled from Actium.

Finding his cause hopeless, Anthony killed himself, and Octavius marched on Alexandria. Here he met Cleopatra, still quite young and beautiful, surrounded by all the luxury of the Egyptian court.

Cleopatra was a very charming and clever woman, and she had been able to persuade both Julius Caesar and Mark Anthony to fight for her. Octavius was however not to be persuaded, and Cleopatra, finding that he meant to take her to Rome as a prisoner, killed herself. The legend is that she allowed herself to be bitten by a poisonous snake, brought to her in a basket of fruit.

The great civilisation of Egypt had lasted for five thousand years, and it has been said of it that it had 'lit the torch of civilisation in ages inconceivably remote, and had passed it on to the peoples of the West.' So remember when you look at a calendar to-day, that it was the idea of an Egyptian scribe, thousands of years ago.

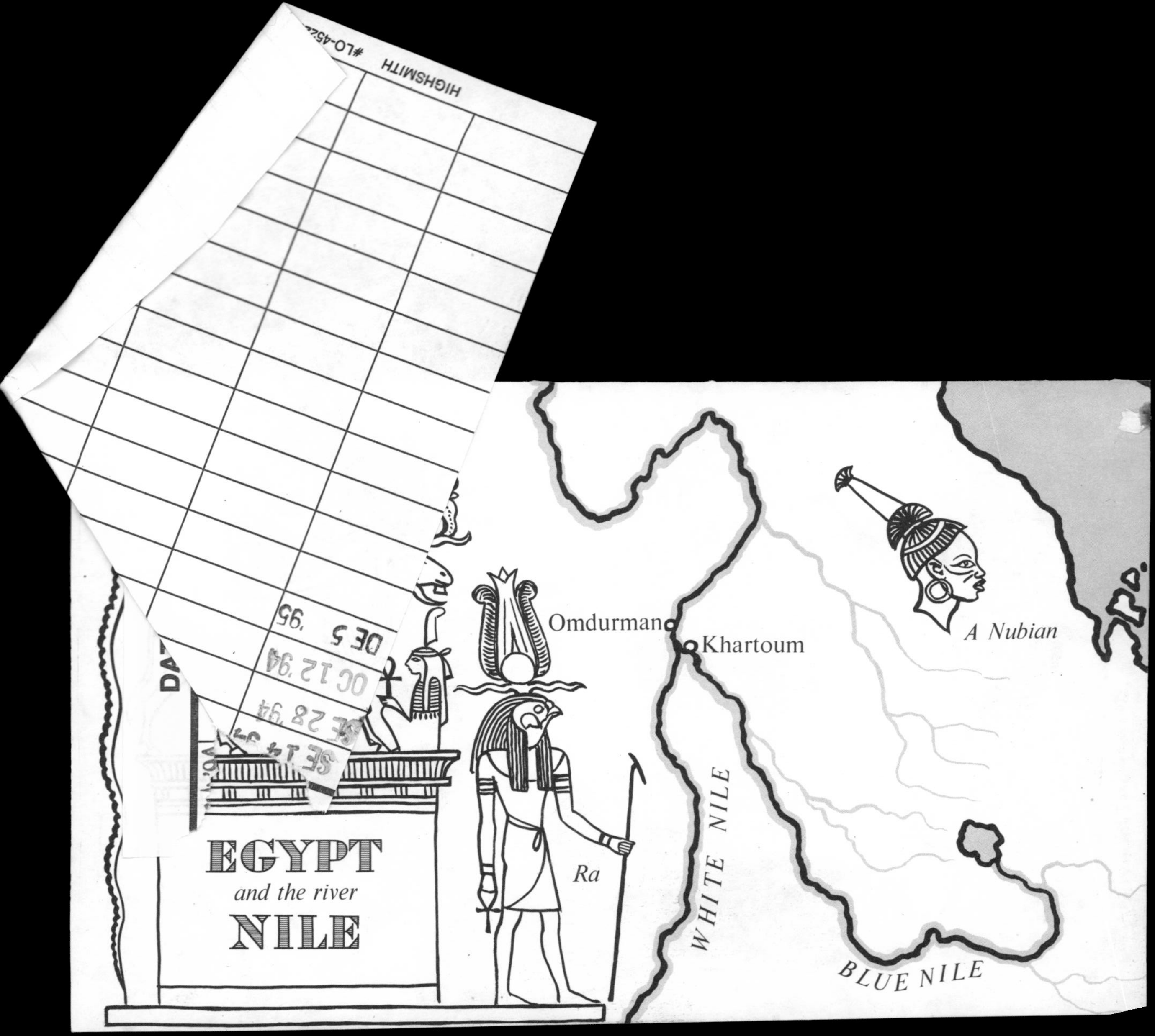
EGYPT
and the river
NILE
Ra
Omdurman
Khartoum
A Nubian
WHITE NILE
BLUE NILE